Melody Fa
Musi *e*

ISHMAEL

Phoenix

Glories like shopping, so it will come as no surprise when I tell you that right in the middle of Glorieland is a large Shopping Centre. There you can find food shops, clothes shops, cake shops, garden shops, even tea shops.

But one thing makes the Glorie Shopping Centre different from any other: whatever shop you enter, you will always be served by a happy smiling face.

This story is about one of the most popular shops in Glorieland, the music shop.

Keef Glorie is really cool. He owns the 'Loud 'n' Quiet Music Shop'. One Friday morning at five minutes before opening time Keef was sitting at his counter drinking a cup of tea, admiring the inside of his brightly coloured shop.

Keef loves music and enjoys gazing at all the different kinds of musical instruments he has for sale. He likes to have as many as possible, so that he has something for everyone. For those who like loud music he's got drum kits, electric guitars and keyboards, trumpets, trombones, saxophones—and of course very loud tambourines. But for those who prefer the quiet, more gentle sounds he has flutes, recorders, acoustic guitars, pianos—and even tambourines with only one or two jingles on.

As Keef opened his door at precisely nine o'clock two Glories bounced in at the same time. The first was Melody Glorie, who was a regular customer and a music teacher. She liked only quiet music. The other was Angus the postman, who was Scottish and really enjoyed the bagpipes, which was about the only instrument that he couldn't see in Keef's shop. While Melody looked around the shop, Angus handed a letter to Keef.

As Keef opened the letter his face lit up. 'Hey, man! It's from my niece, Kylie. She's been asked to play at a concert.' Then his face dropped. 'Oh no! The concert is tomorrow. I won't be able to go, as I'd need to leave straight away to get there in time.'

'So what's your problem?' said Angus. 'Why not just close the wee shop for two days?'

'But tomorrow's Saturday. That's when all the Glories look forward to coming in. I would be letting them down, man.'

'Well, I'm very sorry,' said Angus, still looking around in case Keef did have any bagpipes hidden away somewhere. 'I'm afraid I cannae help you mysel' as I've lots of letters to deliver.'

At that moment Melody bounced up to Keef. 'Excuse me, Keef,' she said in her quiet, posh voice. 'I would be more than happy to look after your shop for you, as I do know quite a lot about music.'

Keef was delighted. 'Wow! Thanks, Melody, that's really cool,' he said, and after giving her a few instructions he left saying that he would be back in time for Monday.

Friday was a pretty quiet day in the Glorieland Shopping Centre, which of course suited Melody nicely. But when half past three came, everything changed. As the school day finished and the weekend was about to begin, excited little bouncing Glories semed to be everywhere, bouncing in and out of every shop. One or two little Miseries were also around, but I'm afraid they never get excited about anything.

Little Glories came bouncing into the music shop, explaining that Keef always let them have a go on some of the instruments, as long as they were careful. So they were soon making more noise than Grandpa Glorie's snoring. And that was loud.

Guitars were twanging,
Drums were banging,
Cymbals crashing,
Glories dashing,
Trumpets blaring,
Melody staring ... with her mouth wide open in amazement, and her hands over her ears.

While all this was going on, Melody didn't notice a young Miserie called Di creep in and sneak beside the counter. Di hated to see the little Glories enjoying themselves.

Frightened that the noise would make her go deaf, Melody raced round the shop taking the instruments and the drum sticks from the excitable young Glories and telling them all to go home and have their tea. The little Glories did as they were told, but asked if they could please come back tomorrow, as Keef always allowed them to come in on a Saturday morning.

Melody put on her best smile and shut the shop door. It was then that she noticed Di Miserie.

'Hello,' said Melody politely. 'May I help you?'

'Well,' said Di, 'I really only wanted to ask you a question.' Knowing that Melody hated loud music, Di saw that she could stir things up and cause trouble.

'I'm a bit surprised at you Glories,' she said. 'Don't you think loud instruments and rock music are wrong? I mean, I'm sure when you sing songs to your Father God, he would hate a lot of noise. Gentle, quiet music is much more proper. Why do you sell all these loud things anyway? They were really made for us Miseries.'

Without waiting for an answer, Di walked out of the shop, pleased that she had just said something that was sure to cause trouble.

Melody thought that maybe Di was right. Suddenly she felt guilty being in the same shop as all these Miserie instruments. She knew she would have to do something about it ... right away!

All Friday night Melody worked at changing the shop. Any instrument that she thought was too loud, or one she thought was only for Miseries, she took out of the shop and hid in the storeroom at the back.

Then Melody went outside to the front of the shop with a ladder, and bouncing up it she stuck a large piece of black cardboard with the word THE on it over the words LOUD 'N'. This changed the name of the shop to 'The Quiet Music Shop'.

Now there was very little left in the shop, but Melody was pleased.

Totally exhausted, she went home to bed.

Saturday came, which, as any shop owner will know, is the busiest day of the week. Mummy Glories were getting the food for the weekend. Daddy Glories were looking round the garden shops. Baby Glories were wanting to go into the toy shops, while teenage Glories were peering in the clothes shops.

But nobody seemed interested in 'The Quiet Music Shop'.

True, the little Glories from the night before had bounced in, but when they saw just a piano, a couple of guitars, a few flutes, dozens of recorders and the two-jingle tambourines, they soon bounced out again. Grandpa Glorie looked in the window hoping to buy a new tambourine for church on Sunday, but seeing they didn't have his favourite loud one he too bounced past. Even those Glories who loved quiet music took one look in the window and didn't bother to go in. The shop looked so empty.

The only one who did go in and thought it was great was Di Miserie. But then she was pleased because of the trouble she was causing.

Melody hoped she'd done the right thing.

Then a strange thing happened. Who should bounce through the door but Keef! He had been to see his niece, but when he arrived he discovered he had read the wrong date and the concert was not till next week. So he hurried back to make sure that Melody was coping with the usual Saturday rush.

Keef stayed cool ... he was speechless! He stared round the shop, not believing his eyes. Then, turning to Melody, he said, 'Say, Melody, like what's happened to the name on my shop? Where are all the instruments? And where are all the Glories who pack my shop every Saturday?'

Melody told Keef about Di and why she felt that loud instruments and Miserie music should not be played by Glories. 'I thought I was doing the right thing,' said Melody, her lip starting to quiver.

Keef was still cool. He knew a lot about music and about Father God. He smiled and asked Melody to sit down on the piano stool. Then he told her that Father God loves all kinds of instruments and all types of music. He doesn't care what sort of noise we make, just so long as we love him. Father God loves variety, and that is why he made us all different. He made us to like different things, including music and instruments.

Melody felt a tear coming into her eye. 'I'm so sorry, Keef,' she said in her posh voice. 'I've tried to make everyone like what I like, instead of letting them choose what *they* like.'

'Never mind, Melody. Hey! Stay cool! No harm done—we all need to learn new lessons every day. So come on and dry those tears. We've got work to do.'

Soon all the loud instruments were brought back in, the sign outside was back as it was, and the shop was full of noise and excited Glories of all ages.

As the day came to an end, and Keef said goodbye to his last customer, he turned and saw a smiling Melody. 'That was a lovely day,' she said, 'even with all that noise.'

'Er, Melody,' Keef said hesitantly, 'Er, I was wondering … it would be really cool if you wouldn't mind …'

Melody guessed what he was trying to say: 'You want me to look after the shop next weekend while you go to the concert? I'd love to. I've decided when it comes to choosing what other people like, instead of letting them choose for themselves, I've changed my tune!'

And with that, they both burst out laughing.